Thomas Penrose

Poems by the Rev. Thomas Penrose

Thomas Penrose

Poems by the Rev. Thomas Penrose

ISBN/EAN: 9783744716307

Printed in Europe, USA, Canada, Australia, Japan

Cover: Foto ©Andreas Hilbeck / pixelio.de

More available books at **www.hansebooks.com**

POEMS

BY THE

Rev. THOMAS PENROSE,

LATE RECTOR OF

BECKINGTON AND STANDERWICK,

SOMERSETSHIRE.

EFFUGIUNT AVIDOS CARMINA SOLA ROGOS.
OVID.

LONDON:

PRINTED FOR J. WALTER, CHARING-CROSS.

M,DCC,LXXXI.

INTRODUCTION.

THOSE who perufe the following Poems, may perhaps find themfelves fufficiently interefted in them, to wifh for fome account of their Author.

HE was the fon of the Reverend Mr. PENROSE, Rector of Newbury, Berks; a man of high character and abilities, defcended from an ancient Cornifh family, beloved and refpected by all who knew him; Mr. PENROSE, jun. being intended for the Church, purfued his ftudies with fuccefs, at Chrift Church Oxon, until the fummer of 1762, when his eager turn to the Naval

and

and Military line overpowering his attachment to his real intereft, he left his College, and embarked in the unfortunate expedition againft Nova Colonia, in South America, under the command of Captain Macnamara. The iffue was fatal.—The Clive, (the largeft veffel) was burnt—And though the Ambufcade efcaped, (on board of which Mr. PENROSE, acting as Lieutenant of Marines, was wounded) yet the hardfhips which he afterwards fuftained in a prize floop, in which he was ftationed, utterly ruined his conftitution. Returning to England, with ample teftimonials of his gallantry and good behaviour, he finifhed, at Hertford College, Oxon, his courfe of ftudies ; and, having taken Orders, accepted the curacy of Newbury, the income of which, by the voluntary fubfcription of the inhabitants, was confiderably augmented. After he had continued in that ftation about nine years, it feemed as if the clouds of

difappointment,

difappointment, which had hitherto overfha-
dowed his profpects, and tinctured his Poetical
Effays with gloom, were clearing away; for he
was then prefented by a friend, who knew his
worth, and honoured his abilities, to a living
worth near 500l. per annum. It came how-
ever too late; for the ftate of Mr. PENROSE's
health was now fuch as left little hope, except
in the affiftance of the waters of Briftol.
Thither he went, and there he died, in 1779,
aged 36 years. In 1768, he married Mifs Mary
Slocock, of Newbury, by whom he had one
child, Thomas, now on the foundation of
Winton College.

MR. PENROSE was refpected for his extenfive
erudition, admired for his eloquence, and
equally beloved and efteemed for his focial
qualities.—By the poor, towards whom he was
liberal to his utmoft ability, he was ve-
nerated to the higheft degree. In oratory and
compofition

compofition his talents were great.—His pencil was ready as his pen, and on fubjects of humour had uncommon merit. To his poetical abilities, the Public, by their reception of his *Flights of Fancy*, &c. have given a favourable teftimony. To fum up the whole, his figure and addrefs were as pleafing as his mind was ornamented.

Such was Mr. Penrose; to whofe memory I pay this juft and willing tribute, and to whom I confider it as an honour to be related.

Multis ille bonis flebilis occidit——
Nulli flebilior quam mihi.

J. P. ANDREWS.

The Grove, Nov. 1781.

CONTENTS.

The

viii C O N T E N T S.

POEMS, &c.

Addreſſed to Three Ladies, on the

DEATH of a favourite PARROQUET.

DEEP from your hallow'd, ſilent ſhades
    Attend, attend, ye tuneful maids ;
        Ye Muſes, haſte along.
Inſpire the tender, moving lay,
For ſurely ſuch a mournful day
        Demands a ſerious ſong.

See where with Pity's force oppreſt,

(While riſing ſorrows heave each breaſt)

Three gentle Siſters weep.

See how they point with ſtreaming eyes,

Where PARROQUETTA ſlumb'ring lies,

Her laſt, eternal ſleep.

In vain the pride of Beauty's bloom,

The vivid dye, the varied plume

O'er her fair form were ſpread :

In vain the ſcarlet's bluſhing ray,

Bright as the orient beam of day,

Adorn'd her lovely head.

Love, beauty, youth, perfection, —— all

Together undiſtinguiſh'd fall

Before the oppoſing Fates.

The liſping tongue, the ſilver hairs,

One common ruin overbears,

One common lot awaits.

Then

Then calm, dear Maids, your woes to peace,

With unavailing forrow ceafe

     Your Favourite to deplore ;

For know, the time will furely come

When *you* (tho' now in beauty's bloom)

     When *you* fhall charm no more.

Learn then your moments to employ

In virtuous love, in Hymen's joy,

     Ere yet thofe moments fly ;

For Fate has doom'd this lot fevere,

The brighteft Belle, the lovelieft Fair,

     Like Parroquetes, muft die.

Written Friday Evening, February 5, 1762, in the Cloyfters of Chrift Church, Oxon;

On being difappointed of going to the

ASSEMBLY at NEWBURY, BERKS.

LOUD howl the winds around this awful pile,
    A dufky light the pale-ey'd moon-beams fhed ;
While I amid the long-drawn cloyfter'd Ile,
    Silent and fad the letter'd pavement tread.

Where, low in earth——ah ! never more to rife,
    Unnotic'd, unregarded, and unknown,
Full many a fhrouded ftudent fleeping lies,
    O'er whom ftill weeps the monumental ftone.

Here,

Here, as I pace the hallow'd gloom along,

  Where at this hour no other foot dares rove,

Quick on my mind what dear ideas throng,

  How heaves my heart, and melts with faithful love.

See, fee my CHLOE rifes to my view,

  In all the pride of youth and Virtue's charms!

Swift as the winds the fair one I purfue,

  But clafp an empty phantom to my arms.

Methinks I fee the dance's circling round,

  The chearful mufick, hark! methinks, I hear!

The viol fweet, and hautboy's gladfome found,

  And fprightly tabor ftrike my wond'ring ear.

But ah! again the pleafing dream is gone;

  Swift as the gales, fee, fee, it flies away;

And leaves me wretched, darkling, and alone

  Amidft this melancholy fcene to ftray.

O! hear,

O ! hear, ye Gods, accept my humble pray'r !

   Grant me, O ! grant my heart's fond, beſt deſire ;

Give to my faithful arms, my conſtant Fair ;

   Give this——nor wealth, nor honours I require.

To

To Miss SLOCOCK.

Written on board the Ambuſcade, Jan. 6th 1763,
a ſhort Time before the Attack of Nova Colonia do Sacramento, in the river of Plate.

THE Fates ordain, we muſt obey;
    This, this is doom'd to be the day;
      The hour of war draws near.
The eager crew with buſy care
Their inſtruments of death prepare,
      And baniſh every fear.

The martial trumpets call to arms,
Each breaſt with ſuch an ardor warms,
      As Britons only know.
The flag of battle waving high,
Attracts with joy each Briton's eye;
      With terror ſtrikes the foe.

                       Amidſt

Amidſt this nobly awful ſcene,
Ere yet fell ſlaughter's rage begin,
  Ere Death his conqueſts ſwell,
Let me to Love this tribute pay,
For POLLY frame the parting lay;
  Perhaps my laſt farewell.

For ſince full low among the dead,
Muſt many a gallant youth be laid,
  Ere this day's work be o'er:
Perhaps e'en I, with joyful eyes
That ſaw this morning's ſun ariſe,
  Shall ſee it ſet no more.

My love that ever burnt ſo true,
That but for thee no wiſhes knew;
  My heart's fond, beſt deſire!
Shall be remember'd e'en in death,
And only with my lateſt breath,
  With life's laſt pang expire.

        And

And when, dear Maid, my fate you hear,

(Sure love like mine demands one tear,

　　Demands one heart-felt figh)

My paft fad errors, O forgive,

Let my few virtues only live,

　　My follies with me die.

But, hark! the voice of battle calls;

Loud thund'ring from the tow'ry walls

　　Now roars the hoftile gun,

Adieu, dear Maid!—with ready feet,

I go prepar'd the worft to meet,

　　Thy will, O God, be done!

ELEGY

E L E G Y

On leaving the River of Plate, after the unfuccefsful
Attack of Nova Colonia do Sacramento, by the
Lord Clive of 64 Guns, the Ambufcade of 40, and
the Gloria of 38; in which the former was unfor-
tunately burnt, with the greateft part of her Crew;
and the two latter obliged to retire in a very fhat-
tered condition.

I.

WHILE the torn veffel ftems her lab'ring way,

  Ere yon blue hills fink ever from my view;

Let me to forrow raife the tribute lay;

  And take of them my long, my laft adieu.

II.

Adieu! ye walls; thou fatal ftream farewel;

  By war's fad chance beneath whofe muddy wave

Full many a gallant youth untimely fell,

  Full many a Britain found an early grave.

III. Beneath

III.

Beneath thy tide, ah! filent now they roll,

    Or ftrew with mangled limbs thy fandy fhore;

The trumpet's call no more awakes their foul!

    The battle's voice they now fhall hear no more.

IV.

In vain the conftant wife and feeble fire,

    Expectant wifh their lov'd return to fee;

In vain their infants' lifping tongues enquire,

    And wait the ftory on their father's knee.

V.

Ah! nought avails their anxious, bufy care;

    Far, far, they lie, on hoftile feas they fell;

The wife's, fire's, infant's joy no more to fhare,

    The tale of glorious deeds no more to tell.

VI.

Learn then, ye Fair, for others woes to feel,

    Let the foft tear bedew the fparkling eye;

When the brave perifh for their country's weal,

    'Tis pity's debt to heave the heartfelt figh.

VII. Ah!

VII.

Ah! glorious DRAKE! far other lot was thine,

　　Fate gave to thee to quell the hostile pride;

To seize the treasures of POTOSI's mine,

　　And sail triumphant o'er LA PLATA's tide.

VIII.

But Providence, on secret wonders bent,

　　Conceals its purposes from mortal view;

And Heaven, no doubt with some allwife intent,

　　Deny'd to numbers what it gave to few.

ELEGY

E L E G Y

To the Memory of Mifs MARY PENROSE,

Who died December 18, 1764, in the
Nineteenth Year of her Age.

HEARD ye the bell from yonder dufky tower?
   Deep, deep it tolls the fummons of the dead;
And marks with fullen note the folemn hour,
   That calls MARIA to her earthy bed.

O! come, ye mournful virgin train, attend,
   With mufing ftep the hallow'd place draw near,
View there your once-lov'd, happy, blooming friend,
   Now filent, flumb'ring on the fable bier.

Come

Come ye, who join'd in friendfhip's facred tie,

    With her engag'd in pleafure's guiltlefs fcene ;

Who fhar'd with her the tender, focial joy ;

    Wove the gay dance, or trod the flow'ry green :

Mark here, O ! mark, how chang'd, how alter'd lies

    The breaft that once with youth's warm tide beat high ;

Read your own fate in her's ;—in time be wife,

    And from her bright example learn to die.

Like drooping lillies cropt by wint'ry wind,

    For fate has doom'd the hour when die *you* muft,

Muft leave the world's fantaftic dreams behind,

    And fleep, and mingle with your parent duft.

Say, are *your* forms with youth's foft graces dreft ?

    Say, are they ting'd with beauty's brighteft bloom ?

So once was her's—by *you*—by all confeft,

    'Till death untimely fwept her to the tomb.

                         Her

Her eyes beam'd out how innocent, how meek!

   At whofe rebuke vice fhrunk abafh'd and pale;

Like vernal Rofes blufh'd her modeft cheek,

   Like them as lovely, and like them as frail.

How was fhe fkill'd the fofteft breafts to move!

   Of hardeft hearts the paffions rough to bend!

How was fhe fkill'd to win the general love!

   How form'd to blefs the hufband or the friend!

With meek-foul'd charity, with pitying hands,

   To mifery oft her little ftore fhe gave;

Now fhe herfelf our flowing tears demands,

   And bids our pious drops bedew her grave.

There on her dufty couch in firm repofe,

   Deaf to our call, the clay-cold flumb'rer lies;

Her beauty faded like the blafted rofe,

   Mute her fweet tongue, and clos'd her radiant eyes.

                             Full

Full many an hour of agonizing pain

   She, patient fufferer, bore her lot fevere;

Well did the anguifh of her foul reftrain,

   Nor dropt one female, one repining tear.

'Midft life's laft pangs Religion lent her aid,

   And wip'd with lenient hand her mifty eyes;

With bleft affurance chear'd the pain-worn maid,

   And bad her hopes high-foaring reach the fkies.

There now, enroll'd with heavenly angels bright,

   Whofe hallow'd hymns their Maker's glories raife,

She fhines, refulgent in the blaze of light,

   And fwells with raptur'd voice the note of praife.

Look down, bleft Saint, O! turn a pitying eye!

   If yet in Heav'n a brother's name be dear:

In the dread hour of danger be thou nigh,

   And lead me far from vice's baneful fnare.

                                          Teach

Teach me, whate'er my future lot fhall be,

To *God's* juft Will my being to refign :

Teach me to fail thro' life's tempeftuous fea :

And like *thy* lateft parting hour be mine.

T O

TO

MY DEAREST WIFE,

ON OUR

WEDDING-DAY.

THE happy Morn's arriv'd at laſt,
  That binds our nuptial union faſt;
And knits our plighted vows in one,
With bonds that ne'er can be undone.
Can I be backward then, to pay
The tribute of this joyful day?
Can I refuſe my voice to raiſe,
And hymn to God the ſong of praiſe?
No—ſurely gratitude demands
This humble action from my hands,
And bids me bleſs that God who gave
Safe paſſage o'er the ſtormy wave,

Who

Who turn'd the fhafts of war afide,

And blefs'd me with fo lov'd a Bride.

O ! be that feafon ne'er forgot,

When Hope itfelf could flatter not,

When doubts were all my foul's employ,

Nor dar'd I paint the prefent joy.

But yet, my Love, be mine the blame,

Thy goodnefs ever was the fame;

The fault was mine, mifguided youth !

When Folly held the place of Truth.

And Vice and Error's fyren fmile,

My artlefs bofom did beguile.

What, though by heedlefs heat mifled

To war, and foreign climes I fled,

Forfook thy love, and peaceful eafe,

And plough'd, long plough'd the Southern feas;

Yet, though unworthy of thy care,

Thy kind, dear, love, purfu'd me there.

And 'midft the battle's horrid ftrife,

Thy tender pray'r preferv'd my life.

C 2

God

God heard thy pray'rs, my heart's lov'd queen,

His fhield proteƈted me unfeen,

His favour kept me fafe from harms,

And lodg'd me in thy faithful arms.

Be 't then my tafk, with grateful breaft

To hufh thy ev'ry care to reft,

And make thee, while thy love furvives,

The happieft of all happy Wives.

Yes, yes, my dear, the nuptial vow

Shall ever bind as ftrong as now ;

My duty I fhall ne'er forego,

No change, no other wifh I'll know ;

But ftill I'll prove to life's laft end,

The kindeft Hufband, trueft Friend.

FLIGHTS

FLIGHTS

OF

FANCY.

VIZ.

THE HELMETS,

CAROUSAL OF ODIN,

MADNESS,

ADDRESS TO THE GENIUS OF BRITAIN.

C 3

THE
HELMETS,
A FRAGMENT.

*The Scene of the following Event is laid in the neighbour-
hood of* Donnington Caſtle, *in a Houſe built after the
Gothic taſte upon a ſpot famous for a bloody encounter
between the Armies of* CHARLES *and the Parliament.*

*The Prognoſtication alludes to Civil Diſſention, which ſome
have foretold would ariſe in England, in conſequence of
the diſputes with America.*

—'TWAS midnight—every mortal eye was clos'd
  Thro' the whole manſion—ſave an antique
  Crone's,
That o'er the dying embers faintly watch'd
The broken ſleep (fell harbinger of Death)
Of a ſick Boteler.—Above indeed
In a drear gall'ry (lighted by one lamp
Whoſe wick the poor departing Seneſchall
Did cloſely imitate,) pac'd ſlow and ſad

The

The village Curate, waiting late to fhrive

The Penitent when 'wake.   Scarce fhew'd the ray

To fancy's eye, the pourtray'd characters

That grac'd the wall—On this and t'other fide

Sufpended, nodded o'er the fteepy ftair,

In many a trophy form'd, the knightly groupe

Of helms and targets, gauntlets, maces ftrong,

And horfes' furniture—brave monvments

Of ancient Chivalry.—Thro' the ftain'd pane

Low gleam'd the Moon—not bright—but of fuch pow'r

As marked the clouds, black, threatning over head,

Full mifchief-fraught;—from thefe in many a peal

Growl'd the near thunder—flafh'd the frequent blaze

Of light'ning blue.—While round the fretted dome

The wind fung furly : with unufual clank

The armour fhook tremendous :—On a couch

Plac'd in the oriel *, funk the Churchman down :

For who, alone, at that dread hour of night,

Could bear portentous prodigy ?——

* Oriel. A projecting Window.

" I hear,

" I hear it," cries the proudly gilded Cafque

(Fill'd by the foul of one, who erft took joy

In flaught'rous deeds) " I hear amidft the gale

" 'The hoftile fpirit fhouting—once—once more

" In the thick harveft of the fpears we'll fhine—

" There will be work anon."————————

————————" I'm 'waken'd too,"

Replied the fable Helmet (tenanted

By a like inmate) " Hark!—I hear the voice

" Of the impatient Ghofts, who ftraggling range

" Yon fummit, (crown'd with ruin'd battlements

" The fruits of civil difcord) to the din

" The Spirits, wand'ring round this Gothic pile,

" All join their yell—the fong is war and death—

" There will be work anon."

————————" Call armourers, ho!

" Furbifh my vizor—*clofe my rivets* up—

                    " I brook

"" I brook no dallying"————————

——————"" Soft, my hafty friend,"

Said the black Beaver, "" Neither of us twain

"" Shall fhare the bloody toil—War-worn am I,

"" Bor'd by a happier mace, I let in fate

"" To my once mafter;—fince unfought, unus'd

"" Penfile I'm fix'd—yet too your gaudy pride

"" Has nought to boaft,—the fafhion of the fight

"" Has thrown your gilt, and fhady plumes afide

"" For modern foppery ;—ftill do not frown,

"" Nor lour indignantly your fteely brows,

"" We've comfort left enough—The bookman's lore

"" Shall trace our fometime merit ;—in the eye

"" Of antiquary tafte we long fhall fhine :

"" And as the Scholar marks our rugged front,

"" He'll fay, this CRESSY faw, that AGINCOURT :

"" Thus dwelling on the prowefs of his Fathers,

"" He'll venerate their fhell.—Yet, more than this,

"" From our inactive ftation we fhall hear

"" The

" The groans of butcher'd brothers, fhrieking plaints

" Of ravifh'd maids, and matrons' frantic howls,

" Already hov'ring o'er the threaten'd lands

" The famifh'd raven fnuffs the promis'd feaft,

" And hoarflier croaks for blood—'twill flow."

——————" Forbid it, Heaven !

" O fhield my fuffering Country !—fhield it," pray'd
The agonizing Prieft.

THE

THE

CAROUSAL OF ODIN.

FILL the honey'd bev'rage high,
　　Fill the fculls, 'tis ODIN's cry:
Heard ye not the powerful call,
Thund'ring thro' the vaulted hall?
" Fill the meath, and fpread the board,
" Vaffals of the griefly Lord."—

　　The portal hinges grate,—they come—
　　The din of voices rocks the dome.
　　In ftalk the various forms, and dreft
　　In various armour, various veft,
　　With helm and morion, targe and fhield,
Some *quivering launces couch*, fome biting *maces wield*:
All march with haughty ftep, *all* proudly fhake the creft.

The

The feaſt begins, the ſcull goes round,

Laughter ſhouts—the ſhouts reſound.

The guſt of war ſubſides—E'en now

The grim chief curls his cheek, and ſmooths his rugged

    brow.

" Shame to your placid front, ye men of death !"

Cries HILDA, with diſorder'd breath.

Hell echoes back her ſcoff of ſhame

To the inactive rev'ling Champion's name.

" Call forth the ſong," ſhe ſcream'd;—the minſtrels

    came ——

The theme was glorious war, the dear delight

Of ſhining beſt in field, and daring moſt in fight.

" Joy to the ſoul," the Harpers ſung,

" When embattl'd ranks among,

" The ſteel-clad Knight, in vigour's bloom,

(" Banners waving o'er his plume)

" Foremoſt rides, the flower and boaſt

" Of the bold determin'd hoſt !"

With

With greedy ears the guefts each note devour'd,

Each ftruck his beaver down, and grafp'd his faithful
    fword.

    The fury mark'd th' aufpicious deed,

      And bad the Scalds proceed.

    " Joy to the foul! a joy divine!

    " When conflicting armies join ;

    " When trumpets clang, and bugles found ;

    " When ftrokes of death are dealt around ;

    " When the fword feafts, yet craves for more ;

    " And every gauntlet drips with gore."—

The charm prevail'd, up rufh'd the madden'd throng,

Panting for carnage, as they foam'd along,

Fierce Odin's felf led forth the frantic band,

To fcatter havock wide o'er many a guilty land.

                          .MADNESS.

M A D N E S S.

S W E L L the clarion, fweep the ftring,
    Blow into rage the Mufe's fires!
All thy anfwers, Eccho, bring,
Let wood and dale, let rock and valley ring,
    'Tis MADNESS' felf infpires.

Hail, awful MADNESS, hail!
    Thy realm extends, thy powers prevail,
Far as the voyager fpreads his 'ventrous fail.
    Nor beft nor wifeft are exempt from *thee*;
    Folly—Folly's only free.

                                  Hark!—

Hark!—To the aftonifh'd ear
The gale conveys a ftrange tumultuous found.
They now approach, they now appear,—
 Phrenzy leads her *Chorus* near,
 And Dæmons dance around.—

 Pride—Ambition idly vain,
 Revenge, and malice fwell her train,—
 Devotion warp'd—Affection croft—
 Hope in difappointment loft—
And injur'd Merit, with a downcaft eye
(Hurt by neglect) flow ftalking heedlefs by.

 Loud the fhouts of MADNESS rife,
 Various voices, various cries,
 Mirth unmeaning—caufelefs moans,
 Burfts of laughter—heart-felt groans—
All feem to pierce the fkies.—

Rough as the wintry wave, that roars

On THULE's defart fhores,

Wild raving to the unfeeling air, ·

The fetter'd Maniac foams along,

(Rage the burthen of his jarring fong)

In rage he grinds his teeth, and rends his ftreaming
  hair.

No pleafing memory left—forgotten quite

All former fcenes of dear delight,

Connubial love—parental joy—

No fympathies like thefe his foul employ,

——But all is dark within, all furious black defpair.

Not fo the love-lorn Maid,

By too much tendernefs betray'd;

Her gentle breaft no angry paffion fires,

But flighted vows poffefs, and fainting, foft defires.

     D   She

She yet retains her wonted flame,

All—but in reafon, ftill the fame.—

Streaming eyes,

Inceffant fighs,

Dim haggard looks, and clouded o'er with care,

Point out to Pity's tears, the poor diftracted Fair.

Dead to the world—her fondeft wifhes croft,

She mourns herfelf thus early loft.—

Now, fadly gay, of forrows paft fhe fings,

Now, penfive, ruminates unutterable things.

She ftarts—fhe flies—who dares fo rude

On her fequefter'd fteps intrude ?—

'Tis he—the Momus of the flighty train—

Merry mifchief fills his brain.

Blanket-rob'd, and antic crown'd,

The mimick monarch fkips around ;

Big

Big with conceit of dignity he fmiles,

And plots his frolics quaint, and unfufpected

  wiles.—

Laughter was there—but mark that groan,

Drawn from the inmoft foul !

" Give the knife, Demons, or the poifon'd bowl,

" To finifh miferies equal to your own."—

Who's this wretch, with horror wild ?—

—'Tis Devotion's ruin'd child.—

Sunk in the emphafis of grief,

Nor can he feel, nor dares he afk relief.—

Thou, fair Religion, waft defign'd,

Duteous daughter of the fkies,

To warm and chear the human mind,

To make men happy, good, and wife.

     To

To point where fits, in love array'd,

 Attentive to each fuppliant call,

 The God of univerfal aid,

 The God, the Father of us all.

Firft fhewn by thee, thus glow'd the gracious fcene,

 'Till Superftition, fiend of woe,

 Bade doubts to rife, and tears to flow,

And fpread deep fhades our view and heaven between.

 Drawn by her pencil the Creator ftands,

 (His beams of mercy thrown afide)

 With thunder arming his uplifted hands,

 And hurling vengeance wide.

Hope, at the frown aghaft, yet ling'ring, flies,

And dafh'd on Terror's rocks, Faith's beft dependence

  lies.

But

But ah !—too thick they croud,—too cloſe they throng,

    Objects of pity and affright !—

Spare farther the deſcriptive ſong—

    Nature ſhudders at the ſight.—

    Protract not, curious ears, the mournful tale,

But o'er the hapleſs groupe, low drop Compaſſion's veil.

ADDRESS

ADDRESS

TO THE

GENIUS OF BRITAIN.

COME, genial spirit, to the earnest call
    Of the true Patriot! wherefoe'er thou art,
O! mark the summons! whether airy borne
In hasty progress, pleas'd thou skimm'st the edge
Of the white bulwark; from the steepy height
Kenning the azure wave, thy own domain;
While on the pebbled shore, scarce heard so high,
The surf breaks foaming. In the distant view
Full frequent pass the womby labourers
Of Commerce, or the gaily-floating pride

Of naval armament.—Or whether deep

In midland occupation glad thou feeft

The various labours of the chearful Loom;

Or Agriculture whiftling at the plough.

Whether the Anvil-notes engage thy ftay,

(Tho' diffonant, yet mufic to the ear

Of him who knows his country;) or the hum

Of the thick crouded Burfe;—come and attend

To Britain's general good! 'Tis not the fhout,

The din of Clamour, drunk with factious rage,

That hails thee; nor the well-diffembling tongue

Of mafk'd Sedition, whofe envenom'd rant

Urges the Croud to madnefs.—Not to thefe

Lift heedful.—'Tis the cool perfuafive voice

Of Reafon wooes.—Quick then with brighteft fmiles

Of mild Humanity adorn thy cheek:

Straight o'er the Atlantic furge, with anxious hafte,

Seek out thy penfive daughter;—once as dear

And

And clofely twining round thy milky breaft,

As was AUGUSTA's felf.—Yet now eftrang'd—

Unhappily eftrang'd ! O by the hand

Take the fair Mourner ; from her tearful eye

Wipe the dim cloud of Sorrow ;—to the throne

Prefent her reconciling.—'Tis a boon,

Moft glorious boon, that to our lateft fons

Will render thy foft influence doubly dear.

Look back, unmov'd by prejudice, look back

To Memory's mirrour.   Pictur'd there we fee

The happy times of Concord ; when the arm

Of Manufacture ply'd the bufy tafk

In various employment :—thro' the eye

Beam'd Chearfulnefs, while all around her fons

Glad Induftry pour'd forth from Plenty's horn

Abundant wealth :—hence to the crouded port

Pafs, Thought, and mark the ants of Commerce ftore

The fpacious hold ; light ran the toilfome day,

Cheer'd

Cheer'd by the hope of the honeſt recompence.

The bark unmoor'd, ſee how the feſtive crew

Urg'd on her ſpeedy courſe; not ſad to quit

Their native ſoil, for in thoſe happier days

AMERICA was home.   There on the ſhore

Stood Expectation, friendly by her ſide

Smil'd Hoſpitality, with open breaſt,

Pleas'd to receive the ſea-beat traveller:

Cheriſh'd, enrich'd that traveller return'd

Bleſſing his double country.—Theſe thy ſweets,

Fraternal intercourſe! But ah! how chang'd,

How ſadly chang'd is now the preſent ſcene,

Pregnant with future griefs! In ſullen ſtate

Beneath the gloomy roofs dull Silence reigns,

Which erſt in better times, reſounded quick

With ſtrokes of active buſineſs: at the forge,

Extinct, in penſive poverty the ſmith

Deſponding leans, incapable to earn

The

The morrow's morfel, while with craving eye

Look up the wife and child, but look in vain,

Faint with defpair.—O'er the deferted loom

The fpider forms her web, poor evidence

Of human floth or want.—Fain would the Mufe

Supprefs the mournful truth; yet forc'd to tell,

She weeps while fhe relates—How are they fall'n,

The fons of Labour, from their profp'rous ftate

Degraded! How, alas! the crouded jail

Swarms with inhabitants, that once had hope

Of fairer evenings to their toilfome morn!

Fill'd is each cell of forrow and of pain

With daily victims:—debtors part, entomb'd

While living, and condemn'd to linger on

To life's laft ebb, unpity'd, unreliev'd:

Part felons, ftamp'd the foes of focial life

By Penury's rough hand, and driven to roam

The fpoilers of the wealthy.—To diftrefs

Abandon'd,

Abandon'd, fcarce the ruin'd mind perceives

It's own peculiar forrows ; but finks down

The creditor's fix'd prey—or to the law

Submits the needful facrifice.—Sad fate

Of thofe, whom Heaven defign'd their country's boaft,

The artizans of fkill.—Nor on the banks

Of venerable THAMES does woe prefide

Lefs perilous ;—THAMES, the prolific fire

Of BRITAIN's wealth : along his winding fhores,

Unoccupy'd, moor'd to deftructive floth,

Whole fleets lie perifhing, a foreft, true,

But ftill a blafted foreft : gloomy ftalks

The unfhipp'd mariner, and meditates

On foreign fervice.—Should fome child of Hope,

Lur'd by the pleafing retrofpect, once more

Spread his broad fail acrofs the well-known fea ;

Should he, amidft the wonders of the deep,

Give way to Fancy's dream, and fondly truft

To

To meet his wonted greeting : how recoils

The vifionary voyage !—Not on the beach

Sit waiting Love and Amity to grafp

His hand, and lead him to their open bower.

No thronging crowds his proffer'd mart attend

With various traffic :—fled—affrighted—fled,

Are all the little deities, that once

Kind, o'er the focial and commercial board

Hung hovering : in their room, fad change ! appear

Stern Refolution, ftoick Stubbornnefs,

And Independence ;—in his hand each holds

His weapon, jealous of the paffing breeze,

And deaf to ancient friendfhip.—In this paufe,

This folemn paufe, that halts 'tween peace and war,

O fly, bleft fpirit, in the royal ear

Whifper forgivenefs ;—'midft the high behefts

Of juftice, let our ever-gracious Sire

Forget not Mercy ;—'tis the brighteft gem

That

That decks the monarch's crown: nor thou, great
    GEORGE,

Difdain the Mufe's prayer ; moſt loyal ſhe

In mild ſubjection down the tide of life,

Steers her light ſkiff.—Urg'd by the plaintive call

Of meek Humanity, O! pardon, now

If warm ſhe pleads her caufe.—The ſavage race,

That prowl the defert, or that range the wood,

Are won to tamenefs by the attentive care

Of the kind gentle keeper.—Shame not man,

Nor fay *his* heart's more fell :—'Tis eaſier far

To footh by tendernefs, than awe by pow'r.

Quit then the bloody purpofe, nor perfiſt

To *conquer*, when the field is fairer gain'd

By reconciling.—To the ungrateful toil

Commiſſion'd, ſhuddering beats the foldier's heart.

Not ſo, when from the plough in eager haſte,

Rous'd by the call to arms, the ſhouting bands

                     Ruſh'd

Rufh'd emulous, reluctant none, nor held

By loves or home ;—each burning to fupply

The wafte of war, and anxious to advance

The common glory.—Spiritlefs now and fad

Embark the deftin'd troops: the veteran brave,

That dauntlefs bore the variegated woes

Of long-protracted war :—the veteran brave,

That won on many a plain the bloody palm

Of Victory, amidft the dying groans

Of flaughter'd thoufands firmly undifmay'd ;

Now hangs in tender thought his honeft front,

Averfe to flay his brother:—at the word,

(Awful, yet *facred* to his patient ear)

He lifts indeed the fteel, while down his cheek

The big drop flows, nor more he dreads the wound

That bores his vitals, than the ftroke he gives.

Say therefore, " *Sword be fheath'd*,"—fair in the fky,

Now cloudy, then the dawn of joy will fpread

Its

Its warm reviving ray—and every eye

That's mifty now with forrow, will grow bright,

And fmile away its tears: the funny beam

Of mild returning Confidence will cheer

The kindred countries:—Commerce, on her couch

Now drooping wounded, then will rear her head,

Charm'd into health;—and from her various ftore

Will cull the fweeteft flowers, and form a wreath

To crown the temples of her PATRIOT KING.

ESSAY

E S S A Y

ON THE

C O N T R A R I E T I E S

O F

P U B L I C   V I R T U E.

SOCIETY, like thong of leather,
   Faſt binds in cluſters men together;
And though it cannot be forgotten,
That ſome are ripe, and ſome are rotten,
Yet,—let it ſtill be underſtood,
They *All* promote the *General Good.*

For this the *Patriot*'s fire arifes,

That glows at every trying crifis,

With each inferior ftrife, and ftir too,

Whence fpring they? but from *Public Virtue.*

Tho' different plans, like ftreams, 'tis true,

By different rills their courfe purfue;

Tho' oft they feem, to mortals blind,

Repugnant to the end defign'd,

Appearing, as by error led,

To flow through many a mazy bed;

Yet ftill at length we fee them glide,

Meand'ring to the common tide.

Smile on, ye grave, in deep derifion,

I fhrink not from my propofition,

But ftill aver *a.l Britons* merit

The praife of *Patriotic Spirit*;

As far as e'er their power can ftretch,

From N—— defcending down to *Ketch.*

That

That ſtateſmen guard the public weal,

We *all* muſt own, for *all* muſt feel:

'Tis their's to watch with ardour keen,

And careful drive the grand machine;

To charm the paſſengers from fretting,

And keep the *whole* from overſetting.

- But ſtill inferior hands may bring

Some little help,—may oil a ſpring,—

May point,—" There, round that corner turn ye,"

And wiſh the folks a pleaſant journey.

All have their uſe,—there's nothing plainer,

From this each traveller's a gainer;

And, tho' the merits be but few,

Let's give to every imp his due.

This ſocial *fire* tho' all poſſeſs,

In ſome there's nothing *blazes* leſs;

So many a cloſe attempt is made,

O'er the bright flame to hold a ſhade,

To

To keep their worth from being known,

While confcience hugs itfelf alone :

As fome of alms will never boaft,

And look *leaft* pleas'd when giving *moft*.

But, Cynics, fpare the odd behaviour,

If well you walk, ne'er blame the Pavior.

Should you, when wand'ring in the night,

Some *Scoundrel* urge to fet you right,

Now, tho' he blafts you with a curfe,

You'll take the *better* from the *worfe*,

Nor think the greeting ill-beftow'd,

If while he *damns*, he fhews the *road*;

But ftraight jog home, no more affrighted,

Than if an honeft *watchman* lighted.

Learn then the *beft* to cull from evil,

As *Saints* take warning by the *Devil*:

And,

And,—if the Mufe, whofe judgment nice is,

Shews *Public Good* in *private Vices,*

The holieft tongue muft ceafe to ftir,

But inftant own without demur,

While modeft matrons ftart at *Drury,*

The *Thief*'s as ufeful as the *Jury,*

Since both the mind ftrong truths imprefs on,

And teach the world an aweful leffon.

Our *various Patriots* then revere,

Their hearts are found, though manners queer:

Tho' fome to outward vifion feem

To fport in *Phrenzy's* antic dream,

The aims of each laborious felf are,

Intended for the *public welfare.*

This glorious end alone purfuing,

They, bold like *Curtius,* laugh at ruin;

For this, if we their fchemes unravel,

They drink, whore, mortgage, game, and travel.

Enthufiaft

Enthufiaft in the paths of *Science*,

BANKS bade the ftormy waves defiance ;

Fair Nature's volume to explore,

He * *fought with feas* unfail'd before,

And earn'd, by *Argonautic* toil,

Frefh honours for his native foil :

Him *Wifdom* lov'd, thus worthy found,

And *Britain* hail'd him as fhe *crown'd.*

But fay—" Can *one Advent'rer's* claim

" Exhauft the trumpet voice of fame ?

" No garland has my country now,

" To bind another pilgrim's brow ?

" Be mine the merit,"—*Florio* cries,

And crofs the *Channel* gaily flies ;

* With fuch mad feas the daring GAMA fought.

ThomSon.

Thro' thick and thin, drives mad and giddy on,

Now here, now there, now in meridian,

(Unlefs perchance when Louis fail,)

A *meteor*—with a fiery tail.

Think you his aim in each manœuvre,

Is but to fcare th' aftonifh'd *Louvre?*

Ah no!—in all the diffipation

He loves the int'reft of his nation,

And, mindful of the Patriot rule,

For our *inftruction*—plays the *fool.*

Connubial faith,—th' unbroken vow,—

How bleft! Who dares to difallow?

Lothario ftrong in this agrees,

And—urges every wife he fees;

Sure—if the attack fhould fail upon her,

The fex is happy in her honour,—

And,—if his ftratagems furprize her,

Her fall may make th' unfteady wifer.

The

The hufband from his doze may ftart,

And, tho' he long difdain'd her *heart*,

May look the thief with vifage fierce on,

Who dar'd defile the flighted *perfon*.

" Draw—draw to fet the matter right,"—

But is *Lothario* wrong to fight?

No,—*Public Virtue* fwells his veins,

Whoever falls,—his country gains :

This none can doubt, your feelings afk, all;

For 'tis a *gain* to lofe a *rafcal*.

When trade unclogg'd can turn it's wheels,

The influence kind the kingdom feels ;

Each hand, in fit degree and meafure,

Contributes to the *public treafure*.

Thefe truths NORTHUMBERLAND convince,

Who lives in juft magnificence,

And,—while his bounty wide diftills,

For *England's welfare*—pays his bills.

But

But different noticns COTTA ftrike,

For why fhou'd *Patriots* judge alike ?

It fhocks his greatnefs to defcribe

How Peafants gall the Courtier's kibe,

An upftart race, that *no one* knows,

Who yet have folly to fuppofe,

That *honeft wealth* is better far

Than *guilt* and *want* beneath a *ftar.*

" Let every man preferve his ftation :

" What's rule—without fubordination ?"

'Till wifer heads confefs the flaw,

And plan a fumptuary law,

Impatient fome redrefs to get,

See COTTA plunges into debt,

(From Bailiffs fafe)—and much commends

This practice to his hungry friends :

So war is wag'd with every trader,

Dear Honour ! left the rogues degrade her :

And

And what contrivance is more fure

To *bumble*,—than to keep them *poor ?*

When in contention fharp of old,

As legendary, tales unfold,

Two * rival deities defign'd

Their choiceft prefents to mankind,

With envy kindling,—warm enforcer!

This gave an *olive*, that a *courfer*.

Thus fome,—as other plans have mifs 'em,

Revere the *vegetable fyftem*,

And think their *virtue* grounded fure

In growth of timber, and—manure.

Hence, up the flope plantations fpread,

And crown the hill's once dreary head ;

Hence, downward as the vale defcends,

The harveft ocean wide extends ;

* Minerva and Neptune.

Glad

Glad *Britain*—how thefe profpects charm her !

Her *Medal* * decks the *Patriot Farmer*,

Who counts his ftock,—and hopes he's ihewn,

His country's riches in his own.

Not fo the 'Squire of boift'rous fpirit,

Who, ftudious of equeftrian merit,

To thrifty care makes no pretences,

But fcours the fields, and breaks the fences.

Vain may the tenant urge his fpeeches,

New till the foil, and mend the breaches,

Yet no reftraint his landlord clogs ;—

Devoted as a *prey* to *dogs*,

He hates ignoble frugal ways,

And—wild in the career of praife,

Cries, as he fpurs his foaming fteed ;

" To *me* *Old England* owes the breed."

---

* Medals given by the Society for the encouraging Arts and Sciences.

Do

Do various loads the nation prefs ?

· 'Tis noble fure to make them lefs :

This *Vigil* does, and labours hard

To cog the *die*, or palm the *card:*

Profufe in *packs*, as round they lie,

He often turns th' applauding eye ;—

And,—though he cheats, thinks nothing of it,

Since his dear country fhares the profit.

Keen Cenfure then her frown relaxes,

Without *confumption* what are *taxes?*

Taxes ! But " why" THERSITES growls,

" Muft every bird be ftripp'd by owls ?

" Shall two or three, in pamper'd eafe,

" Lay contributions as they pleafe,

" While all the reft, in ftation humble,

" Tame bear the lofs,—nor dare to grumble ?"

Peace,

Peace, Snarler,—Know, with fteady foul
The *Patriot* can applaud the whole;
And juftly crowns with equal praife
The man who *levies*, and who *pays*.

'Tis true, the Doctor of finances
By *noftrums* oft his fund enhances:
But then his fkill in phyfic's great,
He knows the ailments of the ftate,
Intent, as fuits the fad difafter,
To cup, prick, purge, or fpread a plaifter.
A *plethora*'s now the cafe, there's needing
Strict regimen, and copious bleeding.
He therefore acts the fubject beft,
Who fcorns the order to conteft;
But claps a calm contented face on,
And yields the moft to fill the bafon.

To

To give his part, thro' various ftages
The *Manufaßurer* engages;
And thinks there's merit at *his* door,
Whofe bufinefs feeds the lab'ring *poor*,
While to the keen *Excifeman*'s eyes
Accumulating *duties* rife.

" Curfe on the drudge's dirty toil,"
Exclaims my haughty lord of foil,
(Tho' oft his title-deeds may reft
Safe in the Us'rer's iron cheft;)
" Unpaid let other calls remain,
" I'll ftill uphold my *menial train* ;
" Oeconomy !—'tis bafe to court her,
" Each * *Footman* is a ftate-fupporter,
" To baulk the caufe a coward's fin is,
" I'll bravely pay the *hundred guineas*."

* New tax on fervants.

Deep

Deep *Bibo* foaks, and boafts the reafon,

" Wine's the beft antidote to *treafon*,

" Our bumpers *large revenues* bring,

" I drink my *Claret* for my *King*."

Yet ftill *his* zeal by far furpaffes,

Who empties firft, then breaks the *glaffes* *.

How *Fungus* glows with Patriot pride;

While *credit* pours an even tide!

Thus buoy'd along, thro' fairy fcenes,

He clubs his fhare to *ways and means*;

At length the *dun*'s inceffant clamour

Dooms every chattel to the *hammer*;

Still there's *decorum* in his fall,

Since now the † *Auction* clofes all.

Smile, *Walpole's ghoft*, untaught to feign,

For *private folly*'s *public gain*:

* New tax on glafs wares.   † Ditto on Auctions.

And

And bid *old Cecil* ſmooth his brow,—
If *England thrives*,—no matter *how*.

   Veſpatian thus, the bee of money,
From every weed could gather honey:
Tho' ſqueamiſh *Titus* leer'd and laugh'd,
The wiſer father bleſt the craft,
And, when his *bags* the *caſh* was ſure in,
Ne'er thought the *tribute* ſmelt of *urine*.

T H E

THE

JUSTICE:

A

CANTATA.

RECITATIVE.

COMPOS'D, the Juſtice ſat in eaſy ſtate;
A croud aſſembling, thunder'd at the gate:
The Porter, to his poſt accuſtom'd long,
Firſt aſk'd the cauſe, then introduc'd the throng:
'Midſt theſe, a Sire enrag'd, two culprits brought,
Her ſwelling waiſt proclaim'd the damſel's fault;
The young Seducer look'd abaſh'd and pale,
While thus the Father urg'd his angry tale:

SONG.

S O N G.

See that wretch, bafe ends purfuing,
 Low has brought my child to fhame—
See in her my honour's ruin,
 Death of honour, death of fame!

Well to match her ripening beauty
 Oft I've form'd the fondeft fchemes;
But this fall, this breach of duty,
 Turns my hopes to idle dreams.——

Curfe the traitor's late repenting—
 Vengeance, vengeance I demand—
War recruits is ever wanting—
 Let him die on foreign land.

R E C I T A T I V E.

He paus'd—for rage his fault'ring voice oppreft—
The magiftrate the trembling youth addreft,

     F   Difpell'd

Difpell'd his terrors with a rifing fmile—
And thus the youth began in artlefs ftile.

SONG.

If the laws I have offended,
    Here for pardon let me fue:
'Twas a crime I ne'er intended,
    Love's the only crime I knew.

Love I plead, (be this prevailing)
    Love in early youth begun;—
We had never known this failing,
    Had yon tyrant made us one.

On our knees we oft have pray'd him,
    Oft have own'd our mutual flame:
Wretched therefore if we've made him,
    On himfelf muft reft the blame.

RECI-

RECITATIVE.

He fpoke, and on his partner turn'd his eye,

Who deep encrimfon'd made this fhort reply.

A I R.

Gracious Sir, this faithful youth

Well has fpoke the voice of truth.

Kind difpenfer of the laws,

Shew compaffion to our caufe—

Hear me on my bended knee—

Spare *bis* life, and pity *me*.

RECITATIVE.

The Judge not long in ufelefs filence fate,

But inftant rofe, and thus announc'd their fate.

A I R.

Relentlefs parent, fince to me

Is now referr'd the laft decree,

Mark and obſerve my juſt command,—
I doom him not to foreign land,
But to a ſentence mild and kind—
Be both at Hymen's altar join'd;
And may their paſſion ne'er decay,
'Till ebbing life ſhall ſink away.

RECITATIVE.

The liſt'ning croud the fair award approv'd,
The youth they favour'd, and the maid they lov'd.
While thanks and praiſes did their tongues employ,
They thus in chorus teſtified their joy.

CHORUS.

Happy pair, who thus have found
 Friendſhip, when you fear'd a foe!
While the year revolves around,
 May your bliſs revolving flow!

Parents,

Parents, to your children's pleafure
  Be your clofe attention paid;
Nor for titles, pomp, or treafure,
  Cut the knot that love has made.

And to thee, thou judge of peace,
  Our beft gratitude is due;
May each couple love like thefe—
  May each Juftice act like you!

THE

THE

HERMIT's VISION.

MILDLY beam'd the queen of night,
    Sailing thro' the grey ferene :
Silver'd by her modeſt light,
    But faintly ſhone the ſolitary ſcene,
With deep'ning ſhadows mixt, and glitt'ring breaks
    between.

    High on a cliffy ſteep, o'erſpread
    With many an oak, whoſe ancient head
    Did in its neighbour's top itſelf inwreath,
And caſt an umbered gloom and ſolemn awe beneath.

                    High

High on a cliffy steep a Hermit sat,

Weighing in his weaned mind

The various turns of mortal fate,

The various woes of human kind;

Meek Pity's pearl oft started in his eye,

And many a prayer he pour'd, and heav'd a frequent

figh.

Silent was all around,

Save when the swelling breeze

Convey'd the half-expiring sound

Of distant-waterfalls, and gently-waving trees.

No tinkling folds, no curfew's parting knell

Struck the sequester'd Anchoret's ear;

Remote from men he scoop'd his narrow cell,

For much he had endur'd, no more he look'd to fear.

F 4   But

But ſtill, the world's dark tempeſts paſt,

What tho' his ſkiff was drawn to ſhore,

And ſhelter'd in retirement faſt,

Yet oft his voyage he'd ponder o'er;

Oft in reflection life's rough ocean view,

How mount the ſtormy waves, how hard to ſtruggle

through !

Before his ſage revolving eyes

Various phantoms ſeem'd to riſe,

Now retreat, and now advance,

And mazy twine the myſtic dance.

Joy led the van, in rapture wild,

Thoughtleſs of the diſtant day;

Sweet *Complacence*, angel mild,

Hied from the frantic pageant far away;

For ſhe was Wiſdom's favour'd child,

In revelry untaught to ſtray.

Joy

Joy led the van—her painted veſt,

 Flowing to th' obſequious wind,

Hope had ſeiz'd, with flutt'ring breaſt,

 And eager tripp'd behind.

Gay ſhe ſtepp'd, till buſy *Fear*

Whiſper'd in her ſtartled ear

" How many a cup is daſh'd with gall,

" How many an evil may befall !"

Aghaſt awhile ſhe heard the ruthful ſong,

Then faſter ſeiz'd the robe, and haſtier danc'd along.

Cloſe *Love* follow'd in the train,

Love, the queen of pleaſing pain :

Placid now in dear delight,

Madd'ning now in deep affright,

And prying keen with jaundic'd eye,

Pierc'd by the ſting of hell-born *Jealouſy*.

        'Twixt

'Twixt *Pride* and *Luft of Grandeur* led,

Next *Ambition* rear'd her head,

By *Phrenzy* urg'd o'er every bar to rife,

And feize the vifionary prize:

Wild as fhe rufh'd, fhe fcorn'd to mark the ground,

Yet many a flip fhe made, and many a fall fhe found.

Pale as the waning moon,

With tear-ftain'd cheek and ftupid gaze,

Withering before life's funny noon,

Grief crept along in fad amaze,

By many a ftroke to keeneft mifery brought,

Now in a fhower diffolv'd, now loft in inward thought.

As the rous'd Tiger gaunt and fell

Kindles into cruel rage,

With

With flashing glare, and murd'rous yell—

Thus *Anger* past th' ideal stage,

Too fierce for wounds or groans to feel,

Onward she sprung, and shook the bloody steel.

While far behind, with silent pace and slow,

Malice was content to go,

Patient the distant hour to wait,

And hide with courteous smiles the blackest *hate*.

Secret long her wrath she'd keep,

'Till time disarm'd the foe, then drove her poniard

deep.

To Malice link'd, as near allied,

Envy march'd with baneful lour;

Detraction halted by her side,

Upheld by *Falsehood's* feeble power.—

" No

"No more!—no more!" the holy Seer exclaim'd,
"Paſſions wild, unbroke, untam'd,
"Muſt ſure the human heart o'erthrow,
"And plunge in all the energy of woe.

"Grant then the boon, all-gracious Heav'n,
"Let reaſon ever take the helm ;
"Left, by unheeded whirlwinds driv'n,
"The pinnace frail ſome guſt may overwhelm !

"Hang out the friendly lamp, that clear
"From Error's perils ſhe may ſafely ſteer ;
"Till death ſhall bid each trial ceaſe,
"And moor the ſhatter'd bark in peace !"

THE

THE

FIELD OF BATTLE.

FAINTLY bray'd the battle's roar
   Diftant down the hollow wind;
Panting terror fled before,
   Wounds and death were left behind.

The War-fiend curs'd the funken day,
   That check'd his fierce purfuit too foon;
While, fcarcely lighting to the prey,
   Low hung, and lour'd the bloody moon.

The

The Field, fo late the hero's pride,

    Was now with various carnage fpread;

And floated with a crimfon tide,

    That drench'd the dying and the dead.

O'er the fad fcene of drearieft view,

    Abandon'd all to horrors wild,

With frantic ftep *Maria* flew,

    Maria, Sorrow's early child;

By duty led, for every vein

    Was warm'd by Hymen's pureft flame:

With *Edgar* o'er the wintry main

    She, lovely, faithful, wanderer, came.

For well fhe thought, a friend fo dear

    In darkeft hours might joy impart;

Her warrior, faint with toil, might chear,

    Or foothe her bleeding warrior's fmart.

Tho'

Tho' look'd for long—in chill affright,

   (The torrent burſting from her eye)

She heard the ſignal for the fight—

   While her ſoul trembled in a ſigh—

She heard, and claſp'd him to her breaſt,

   Yet ſcarce could urge th' inglorious ſtay;

His manly heart the charm confeſt—

   Then broke the charm,—and ruſh'd away.

Too ſoon in few—but deadly words,

   Some flying ſtraggler breath'd to tell,

That in the foremoſt ſtrife of ſwords

   The young, the gallant *Edgar* fell.

She preſt to hear—ſhe caught the tale—

   At every ſound her blood congeal'd;—

With terror bold—with terror pale,

   She ſprung to ſearch the fatal field.

                     O'er

O'er the fad fcene in dire amaze

    She went—with courage not her own—

On many a corpfe fhe caft her gaze—

    And turn'd her ear to many a groan.

Drear anguifh urged her to prefs

    Full many a hand, as wild fhe mourn'd;—

—Of comfort glad, the drear carefs

    The damp, chill, dying hand return'd.

Her ghaftly hope was well nigh fled—

    When late pale *Edgar*'s form fhe found,

Half-bury'd with the hoftile dead,

    And bor'd with many a grifly wound.

She knew—fhe funk—the night-bird fcream'd,

    —The moon withdrew her troubled light,

And left the Fair,—tho' fall'n fhe feem'd—

    To worfe than death—and deepeft night.

MORTA-

MORTALITY.

'TWAS the deep groan of death
   That ſtruck th' affrighted ear!
The momentary breeze,—the vital breath
Expiring ſunk!—Let Friendſhip's holy tear—
   Embalm her dead, as low he lies.—
To weep another's fate, oft teaches to be wiſe.

   Wiſdom ! ſet the portal wide,—
   Call the young, and call the vain,
   Hither lure preſuming Pride,
   With Hope miſtruſtleſs at her ſide,
And Wealth, that chance defies, and greedy Thirſt of
   Gain.

G   Call

Call the group, and fix the eye,—

Shew how awful 'tis to die.—

Shew the portrait in the duft :—

Youth may frown—the picture's juft,—

And tho' each nerve refifts—yet yield at length they

    muft.

Where's the vifage, that awhile

Glow'd with glee and rofy fmile ?

Trace the corpfe,—the likenefs feek—

    No likenefs will you own.

Pale's the once focial cheek,

And wither'd round the ghaftly bone.

Where are the beamy orbs of fight,

    The windows of the foul ?

No more with vivid ray they roll—

    Their funs are fet in night.

Where's

Where's the heart, whofe vital power
    Beat with honeft rapture high,—
That joy'd in many a friendly hour,
    And gave to mis'ry many a figh?—

Froze to a ftone!—And froze the hand
    Whofe grafp affection warm convey'd;
Whofe bounty fed the fuppliant band,
    And nourifh'd Want with timely aid.

Ah! what remains to bring relief,—
To filence agonizing grief,—
To foothe the breaft in tempeft toft,
That thrilling wails in vain the dear companion loft?

    'Tis the departed worth, tho' fure
    To gafh the wound, yet works the cure:—

                'Tis

'Tis Merit's gift alone to bloom
O'er the dread horrors of the tomb;
To dry the mourner's pious ftream,
And foften forrow to efteem.

Does Ambition toil to raife
Trophies to immortal praife?
Truft not, tho' ftrong her paffions burn,
Truft not the marble's flattering ftile,
—Tho' Art's beft fkill engrave the urn—
Time's cank'ring tooth fhall fret the pile.—

FRIEND-

FRIENDSHIP.

DISTILL'D amidſt the gloom of night,
  Dark hangs the dew-drop on the thorn;
'Till, notic'd by approaching light,
  It glitters in the ſmile of morn.

Morn ſoon retires, her feeble pow'r
  The ſun outbeams with genial day,
And gently, in benignant hour,
  Exhales the liquid pearl away.

Thus on Affliction's ſable bed,
  Deep ſorrows riſe of ſaddeſt hue;
Condenſing round the mourner's head,
  They bathe the cheek with chilly dew.

G 3   Tho'

Tho' *Pity* fhews her *dawn* from Heaven,

    When kind fhe points affiftance near ;

To *Friendfhip*'s *Sun* alone 'tis given

    To foothe and dry the mourner's tear.

T H E

THE

CURATE.

A FRAGMENT.

I.

O E'R the pale embers of a dying fire,
His little lampe fed with but little oile,
The Curate fate (for fcantie was his hire)
And ruminated fad the morrowe's toil.

II.

'Twas Sunday's eve, meet feafon to prepare
The ftated lectures of the coming tyde;
No day of refte to him,—but day of care,
At manie a Church to preach with tedious ride.

Before

III.

Before him fprede, his various fermons lay,
  Of explanation deepe, and fage advice ;
The harveft gained from manie a thoughtful daye,
  The fruit of learninge, bought with heavy price.

IV.

On thefe he caft a fond but tearful eye,
  Awhile he paufed, for forrowe ftopped his throte,
Arroufed at lengthe, he heaved a bitter fighe,
  And thus complainde, as well indeed he mote :

V.

" Hard is the fcholars lot, condemned to fail
  " Unpatronized o're life's tempeftuous wave ;
" Clouds blind his fight ; nor blows a friendly gale,
  " To waft him to one port—except the grave.

" Big

VI.

" Big with prefumptive hope, I launch'd my keele,

" With youthful ardour, and bright fcience fraughte;

" Unanxious of the pains, long doom'd to feel,

" Unthinking that the voyage might end in noughte.

VII.

" Pleafed on the fummer-fea I daunced a-while,

" With gay companions, and with views as fair;

" Outftripp'd by thefe, I'm left to humble toil,

" My fondeft hope abandon'd in defpair.—

VIII.

" Had my ambitious mind been led to rife

" To higheft flights, to Crofier and to Pall,

" Scarce could I mourn the miffinge of the prize,

" For foaringe wifhes well deferve their fall.

" No

IX.

" No tow'ring thonghts like thefe engag'd my breaft,

  " I hoped (nor blame, ye proud, the lowly plan)

" Some little cove, fome parfonage of reft,

  " The fcheme of duty fuited to the man ;

X.

" Where, in my narrow fphere fecure, at eafe,

  " From vile dependence free, I might remain,

" The guide to good, the counfellor of peace,

  " The friend, the fhepherd of the village fwain.

XI.

" Yet cruel fate denied the fmall requeft,

  " And bound me faft, in one ill-omened hour,

" Beyond the chance of remedie, to refte

  " The flave of wealthie pride and prieftlie pow'r.

" Oft

XII.

" Oft as in ruffet weeds I fcour along,

" In diftant chappels haftilie to pray,

" By nod fcarce noticed of the paffing thronge,

" 'Tis but the *Curate*, every childe will fay.

XIII.

" Nor circumfcribed in dignitie alone

" Do I my rich fuperior's vaffal ride ;

" Sad penurie, as was in cottage known,

" With all its frowns, does o'er my roof prefide.

XIV.

" Ah ! not for me the harveft yields its ftore,

" The bough-crown'd fhock in vain attracts mine eye;

" To labour doom'd, and deftin'd to be poor,

" I pafs the field, I hope not envious, by.

" When

XV.

" When at the altar furplice-clad I ftand,

  " The Bridegroom's joy draws forth the golden fee;

" The gift I take, but dare not clofe my hand;

  " The fplendid prefent centres not in me."

DONNING.

DONNINGTON CASTLE.

BLOW the loud trump of war,—wide to the gale
  Unfurl the painted banner,—from the breaſt
Tear the mild ſympathies of charity,
And fan the battle's fire.—What boots it now
If Briton fight with Briton!——Is there one
To whom theſe ſhouts give joy? can there be one
So ſteel'd, ſo frantic with envenom'd rage
Of party feud, as to forego the mark
Of fair humanity?—Reckleſs to pluck
The bloſſoms from the olive, and dye them red
Deep in a brother's blood?—If ſuch there be

(Cain's

(Cain's heir legitimate) O let him turn

His fierce eye to the defolated crown

Of many a batter'd hill,—to many a heap

Of ruins fcatter'd thro' this worried land,

Scenes once of civil ftrife, but now become

Familiar to the lowlieft village fwain.

If there be one within this fertile vale

(Fertile thro' peace) who yearns for acts of blood,

Direct his view, Divine Benevolence!

To yonder awful, but inftructive pile

Of grandeur fallen,—on the indented ridge

Stands eloquent the fiege-worn monitor,

That fpeaks from every ftone;—from ev'ry wound

That bor'd its ftrong, yet vain refifting fide

Truth tells a folemn leffon.—To the ear

Of warm poetic fancy fpeaks the ghoft

Of Chaucer, prime of bards, who caught the fouls

Of

Of *Ladies* born for love, and e'en could lure

For some soft season the stout rugged hearts

That fill'd the steel-clad warriors of his age,

And made them listen to his Syren voice

Half-angry—yet unwilling to be gone.

'Tis *Chaucer* hails, from the drear ivy'd tower,

The gaze of idle visitants,—but once

The seat of all the Muses,—where his court

.Kept *Phœbus*, gladden'd at the pow'rful call

That woo'd him to our Albion :—round him play'd

Old Comus jocular, with many a glee

Promoting social laughter ;—many a Grace

Stole in amidst the chearful throng, and sooth'd

The bashful maiden, while with blushing joy

She hearken'd to her all-accomplish'd *Knight*.

Chaucer, the prime of bards !—with festive song

Oft has he charm'd the variegated groupe

Within

[96]

Within yon ancient walls,—walls that no more

Refound with jocund minftrelfy.—The owl

There fhrieks her ominous note, the raven hoarfe

Joins in the horrid difcord: direful change!

POVERTY

POVERTY.

HIE thee hence! thou fpectre foul,
    Fiend of mifery extreme;
Hence! nor o'er yon dwelling fcowl
With blafting eye, while to thy haggard fcream
The midnight wolf accords his famifh'd howl,
And madd'ning wretches loud in agony blafpheme.

Hence!—from the artlefs bard keep wide aloof—
    Fly rather to *his* hated roof,
    Who, deaf to Mercy's foft controul,
    Can fteel with rugged edge the foul:
Plund'ring, unmov'd the orphan's cry can hear,
Or from the widow'd lip the fcanty morfel tear:—

But paſs *him* by, the *wooer* mild

Of *Genius*, friend to all, *Nature's ingenuous child.*

    Conſtant toil, and coarſeſt fare,

    Long indeed the village hind

    In ſilent apathy may bear,

While o'er his brow Health's roſy wreath is twin'd :

    While his paſſions ſluggiſh flow,

    Borne on life's pacific round ;

    Nor aims his higheſt wiſh to know

Beyond the hamlet's pale, his grandſire's fartheſt

    bound.

    Yet, rous'd to feeling, much he mourns his lot,

    When the pale viſage of Diſeaſe

    Frowns on his humble *cot,*

When ſinks his drooping front, and bend his feeble

    knees.

                              There,

There, oft, unheeded on the ground,

    May Sicknefs, Age, and Want be found,

United *all* in one forlorn abode,

Of grief each fingly own'd a melancholy load.

    From the damp and earthy bed

The fufferer lifts his aching fight in vain :—

    Defpair hangs weeping o'er his head :

Sad pallet this for eafe! fad comforter in pain!

    Fly, ye rich, unbidden fly,

Pour your oil, and pour your wine :

    Wipe from tears the mifty eye;

Charity's a ray divine—

A ray that lights the foul with brighteft beam to fhine.

    Why withhold the little boon ?

    Seems it much, ye fons of wealth,

        H 2   Glitt'ring

Glitt'ring moths of funny noon—
    Plum'd with gold of joy and health?
O think! a blaft may come, yourfelves may perifh foon!

    Yet, different in this common ftate,
      What different care attends your happier fate!
      Fading you may fure receive
All wayward fancy craves, all foothing art can give:
      While, with equal wants oppreft,
    The child of Mifery heaves his lab'ring breaft,
      Cheer'd by no kind affifting powers,
Scarce with fuch crumbs fuftain'd as hungry Health devours.

    Melt, in foft compaffion melt,
    Ye gentle, wail th' unletter'd peafant poor:
    Yet keener far, as more feverely felt,

Does

Does Penury haunt th' ill-omen'd fcholar's door;
He calls for all your tears ; give thefe, if nothing more.

Warm'd his foul with genial flame
In youth's gay fpring was bid to rife,
To pant for fcience, thirft for fame,
And hope fair Merit's golden prize.

Much he hop'd, for many a tale
Of praife was echo'd to his ear ;
Full many a promife (flatt'ring gale !)
Foretold the wifh'd-for port was near.

Awhile it blew,—then dy'd away,
Like breezes with declining day,
And left him, wond'ring wretch ! forfaken quite,
In Poverty's dead calm, and Difappointment's night.

H 3   What

'What avails th' expanded mind,

Tutor'd in the choiceſt lore?

The ſuffering *body* lags behind,

Nor lets the riſing ſpirit ſoar:

Call'd home,—what Stoic pride the ſoul can ſteel,

When every ſinew's rack'd, and every nerve muſt feel?

What avails the glowing heart,

The eye that gliſtens at diſtreſs;

The wiſh all bleſſings to impart,

Or make at leaſt a brother's ſorrow leſs?

From Trouble's ſpring the deepeſt draught *he* drew,

Who mourns his own hard lot, and weeps for others too.

At the ſad miſtaken gate

When the maim'd veteran takes his ſuppliant ſtand,

Struck with the hapleſs warrior's ſtate,

Sudden the pitying tenant gives his hand.—

—'Tis

——'Tis empty—See! his lids o'erflow,
To fend undol'd away the hoary fon of woe.

Love too—for in the lowlieft cell
　　Chafte love with pureft flame may dwell—
　　His love—what forer can befall?
Is doom'd to four its fweets, and dafh his cup with gall.

Before the hufband's and the father's eyes
　　Stormy clouds in profpeft rife,
The future orphan's cry, the widow's groan;
　　Thefe and more he makes his own—
For ah! the faithlefs world by him too well is known.

For thefe the homely robe, the fcanty board,
　　While life in toil is ling'ring on,
　　The drudge of fcience may afford:—
But where's the friend will cheer, when that poor life
　　is gone?

No friend may rife, but many a foe

 Will deck his vifage with a fmile,

 Will hide in fofteft words the bafeft guile,

And, while he foothes the moft, will ftrike the deepeft

 blow.

 Hence the pang, and hence the tear, .

 When his daughter's rip'ning bloom

 Swells into agony his fear

Of the fell fpoiler's den—fair Virtue's early tomb.

THE

THE

HARP.

BORNE on Fancy's wing along,
  High foars the bard's enraptur'd foul:
Round him floats the joy of fong,
Round him airs extatic roll:
Refiftlefs charm! each fwelling vein
Owns the accuftom'd flame, and throbs to pour the
  ftrain.

Spirit of Offian!—thro' the gloom
  Of ages deepen'd into night,
See it burfting from the tomb,—
  O'er it gleams a holy light!

See!

See ! it waves its mafter-hand;

Affembling o'er the heath quick glide the minftrel
band.

They wake the fleeping chords !—the magic tone

(That footh'd the dying warrior's groan,

That lur'd to fing the lateft breath,

And mock'd with fmiles the frown of death,)

Ideal, now renews the powerful fpell;

The lift'ning fhades, a grifly hoft,

Spring from the narrow cell,

And hail with lengthen'd fhout th' enchanter's mighty
ghoft.

Thine too, Cadwallo ! whom to fave

In vain the heavenly fcience fu'd,

Starts from *Arvon*'s rocky grave

With bloody ftreams embru'd.

Bound

Bound in the brotherhood of woe,

The *Druid* choir unites, their tears harmonious flow.

Wild as they fweep th' aerial lyre,

Arrefting faft the paffive ear,

Fiercer glows the poet's fire,—

O melody belov'd! O art for ever dear!

Ruthlefs tyrant,—yield to fate :—

Nor Folly's fcorn, nor Rancour's hate,

Tho' op'ning wide the fluice of gore,

Could quench the fkill divine, could drown the myftic

lore.

Long !—long indeed 'twas mute! thy feeble prey,

Fall'n the hoary minftrels lay :—

While, fick'ning o'er the mournful ground,

The conquer'd bands oft turn'd the ear in vain :

No

No more was heard the foul-infpiring found,—

—But, fafter in Defpair's fad fetters bound,

Each hung his head amaz'd, and dragg'd the fervile
    chain.

    Wint'ry, thus the ftorm of war

Froze into floth the captive mind :

    'Till growing Freedom burft the icy bar,

And loos'd the arts that hell for ever ftrove to bind.

D I S A P-

DISAPPOINTMENT.

A FRAGMENT.

I.

* * * * * *

* * * * * *

* * * * * *

* * * * * *

II.

So figh'd *Horatio*, on a tomb reclin'd,

    Beneath a mould'ring chapel's ivy'd wall:

His ruin'd hope o'ergloom'd his fickly mind,

    And bade the head to droop—the tear to fall.

III. *Horatio*

III.

Horatio, to whofe lot was not deny'd
    Keen Senfibility with *all* her woes:
By many a *painful* teft his heart was try'd;
    His was the *thorn,* while *others* won the *rofe.*

IV.

Yet, why fhould thorns his honeft breaft invade,
    Since all the Charities were fondled there?
Why fhould thy feat, Benevolence, be made
    The haunt of haplefs Grief, and pining Care?

V.

Fill'd with an ample foul, that would adorn
    Fair Independence, he began his day:
Full many a *promife* fmil'd upon his morn:
    Morn chang'd to eve,—each promife dy'd away.

VI. He

VI.

He wifh'd,—nor can you call his wifhes bold ;
   He hop'd,—for fure his friends were not a few
He hop'd,—for many a flattering tale was told,
   And the fafe harbour pointed to his view.

VII.

The foft delufion play'd before his fight
   Juft to miflead ;—for foon, alas! he found
His dawn of joy o'ercaft with fudden night,
   His air-built vifion totter'd to the ground.

T H E

THE

N A V Y.

A FRAGMENT.

DOWN the variegated fide
    Of *Edgecombe*'s far-recorded Knowl,
(Joy of Nereids, *Cornwall*'s pride)
Where Art extends her mild controul
But juft to check what Nature's liberal hand
Has fpread in gay luxuriance wide
Of rocks, dells, groves, a fairy land;
The Mufe, aftonifh'd, trac'd her ling'ring way,
Unfettled what to leave, and wond'ring where to ftay.

FRAG-

FRAGMENT.

SCRANNEL, pipe of scanty tone,
 Yield the prize, and yield it due—
Pan, if here, must surely own,
 From thee no heavenly rapture grew—
  Thine's the frolic to advance,
  Rustic joy, and rustic dance.—
  Merry glee, in many a round
  Tripping o'er the daisy'd ground,
  Prais'd thy note, while rival feet
  Strove thy movements fast to meet.—

I   A TALE.

A

T A L E.

Founded on an Incident at St. Vincent's
Rocks, 1779.

H IG H on the cliff's tremendous fide,
　　That frowning hangs o'er Avon's tide,
　Three laffes chanc'd to ftray:
To pluck the cafual flow'rets bent,
Regardlefs of the rough afcent,
　They wound their dangerous way.

'Till, flowly mounted to the height,
They turn'd their view in wild affright,

　　　　　　　　　　　　And

And fhudd'ring mark'd the fteep :
O ! then, what grief bedew'd each eye,
To think one flip, one ftep awry,
    Might plunge them in the deep !

A Prieft, whom foft emotions prefs
To fuccour damfels in diftrefs,
    That inftant trod the fhore ;
With happy ftrength and fteady pace
Safe to the rock's time-moulder'd bafe
    Each trembling nymph he bore.

Learn then this truth ;—the carelefs hour
May feek a gay, but treacherous flower,
    Whofe honey turns to gall :
While the kind parfon's timely aid
May refcue many a tott'ring maid,
    And——fave from many a fall.

EARLY

EARLY GREY HAIRS.

O'ER my head, e'en yet a boy,
   Care has thrown an early fnow—
Care, be gone !—a fteady joy
   Soothes the heart that beats below.

Thus, tho' Alpine tops retain
   Endlefs winter's hoary wreath;
Vines, and fields of golden grain,
   Cheer the happy fons beneath.

BAGATELLE.

BAGATELLE.

EVERY hour a pleasure dies—
  What is thought, but nurse to sorrow?—
He, that wishes to be wise,
  Lives to day, and mocks to-morrow.

On the BIRTH-DAY of Miss S. C.

I.

EXULTING on the balmy gale,
  When Flora wakes the May-dew morn,
The Rose-bud all with rapture hail,
  Sweet glory of the loveliest thorn!
Each day refines the rich perfume—
  Glad Flora smiles—The zephyr blows—
While op'ning with a gradual bloom
  The favourite ripens to a Rose.

II. Thus

II.

Thus in our Sufan's shape and face,
  Respondent to her angel soul,
The growth of each attractive grace
  We mark—as annual circles roll.
Advance, ye years !—And ev'ry charm,
  Which Venus boasts, shall sure be given;
While soft'ring Friendship joys to form
  Her mind, the fairest work of Heaven.

VERSES

VERSES

Occafioned by hearing that a Gentleman at the HOTWELL, BRISTOL, had written Satirical Verfes on a LADY. 1779.

FOR nobler purpofes defign'd
   Than puny war to wage,
What caufe can fink a hero's mind
   To worfe than woman's rage?

What female fault can roufe the foul
   To dip the ranc'rous quill?
How juftify th' invenom'd fcroll
   One female fame to kill?

If

If frailty aims the flight offence,
  What man perceives the fmart ?
O ! let not bravery and fenfe
  Return the feeble dart.

O'er the foft fex love gladly throws
  Its adamantine fhield,
And few are ever known their foes,
  Or try th' inglorious field.

Thus on the form of Beauty's queen
  One only Greek was found,
Rough Diomed, with weapon keen,
  Who dar'd inflict a wound

———————

OSSA QUIETA, PRECOR, TUTA REQUIESCERE IN
  URNA,
ET SIT HUMUS, CINERI, NON ONEROSA, TUO.

Ovid.

THE END.